Be Careful

By Joel Brown

Illustrated by
Garrett Myers

Rapier Kids
A Division of Rapier Publishing Company

Be Careful
Copyright © 2015

By Joel Brown
Illustrated by Garrett Myers

ISBN 978-0-9966083-3-6
Library of Congress Control Number 2015949179

Published by
Rapier Publishing Company
260 W. Main Street, Suite #1
Dothan, Alabama 36301

www.rapierpublishing.com
Facebook: www.rapierpublishing@gmail.com
Twitter: rapierpublishing@rapierpub

Book Cover Design: Garrett Myers/ Book Layout: Rapture Graphics

Follow all the Current Zoom-Boom Book Series by Joel Brown:

Zoom-Boom the Scarecrow and Friends
Be Tidy, or Not?
Be Careful

Thank you for buying this book. It is important to me that my stories are humorous and educational for the adults and children that read them. I was God-inspired to write the Zoom-Boom series of books for my granddaughters. I wanted the stories to be read mainly at bedtime, so that the time shared during those moments would invite questions from the children and discussions about the stories with the parents. I wanted children to have happy thoughts and dreams at bedtime and what better way to do that than to have the comfort and love of a parent reading a *"Zoom-Boom"* bedtime story. With such busy schedules, we often miss opportunities to make our children feel safe and secure while they are awake. So, a soothing voice, a bedtime story, a hug and a kiss before going to sleep is a wonderful way to end the day. This way, the children can feel that *Zoom-Boom* can handle any "Green Eyed Monster" that might be hiding under the bed or in the closet, should they awaken during the night after a nightmare. I hope that you and your children will enjoy reading these stories, as much as I enjoyed writing them.

Author
Joel Brown

One of the most important things that you can be is...SAFE!

Your parents can't be with you every moment,

so it is important that you listen to them about being SAFE,

when they are not with you.

And one place you REALLY need to be safe is away from home.
Always make sure that you hold your parent's hand
when there is a lot of traffic around.
Never pull away from your parents and do not wander off
to watch nature (butterflies, flowers, insects, etc.)
out of the view of your parents.

You could get HURT and that would make everyone very sad, especially Zoom-Boom.

He wants you to always be careful and to always listen to what your parents tell you to do.

Because if you do not listen to your parents or an adult about safety, then "TROUBLE, TROUBLE, TROUBLE" might find you, and no one wants to be in trouble, right?

Carrie Careless doesn't listen.

She is very smart, but she doesn't pay attention either.

Zoom-Boom spends most of his time rescuing her.

Carrie Careless rides the school bus to school with her friends.
When it is time to get off of the bus,
she never looks before crossing the street. Zoom-Boom got there
just in time to save her!

(Oh, dear!) ZOOM, BOOM and away he went.
In a FLASH he picked up Carrie Careless and safely carried her back
to the sidewalk before anyone noticed.

Carrie Careless was not thinking about safety.

She was talking and not paying ATTENTION at the time.

We must be careful around cars, buses and trucks!

Carrie Careless had dropped her school book in the street and was afraid that she would get in trouble for losing it.
She thought that it was okay to go back out into the street to get it.
(Oh, dear!)
ZOOM, BOOM and off he went and got her book out of the street!

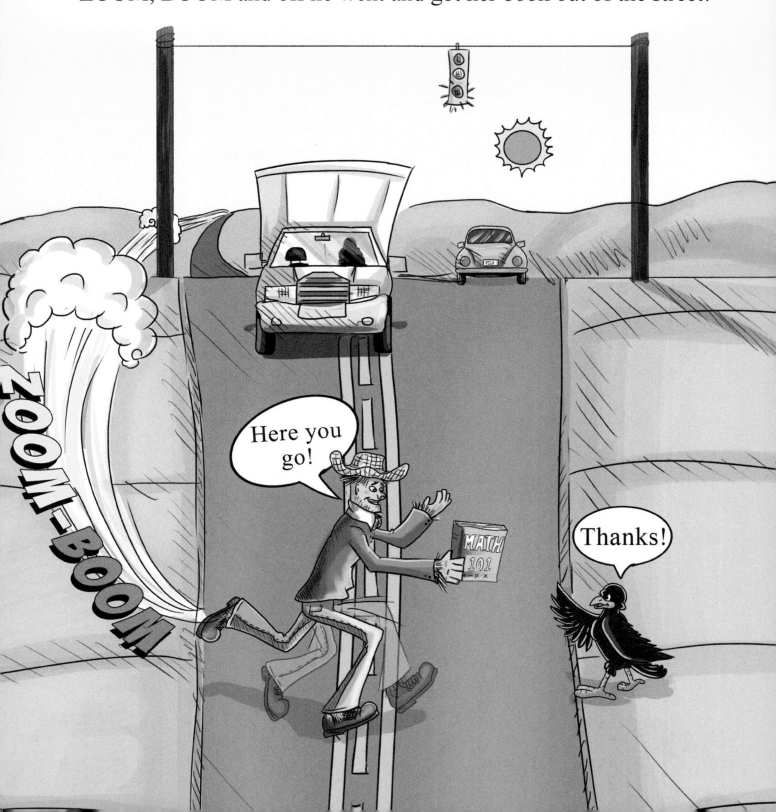

Boys and girls, "NEVER, NEVER, NEVER" go out into the street

if you drop something or it rolls away from you!

THAT IS VERY DANGEROUS!!

If you drop something like a book, your coat, or your money ($$$),

or anything in the street and you have already safely crossed over

to the other side, LEAVE IT THERE!

DO NOT GO BACK TO GET IT!

You could get hit and hurt very badly!

BOOK STORE

You can get another book.

DEPT. STORE

You can get another coat.

Someone will give you some more money ($$$).

But... you can not get another YOU!

And NEVER cross the street, unless the School Crossing Guard,

your parents or a caring adult that you know tells you that it is okay

to cross the street at the crosswalk or traffic signal.

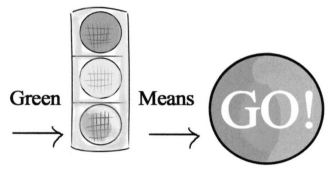

Green → Means → GO!

Zoom-Boom can not come to your rescue,

like he did for Carrie Careless!

WALK

Carrie Careless was very grateful, but it wasn't very long
before she was "careless" again!
This time she didn't hold onto the handrail while going down the steps
and she tripped. Zoom-Boom came to her rescue again!

*** Please hold onto the handrails, when going up or down the stairs!***

Everyone else was holding onto the handrail, except Carrie Careless.

She never saw the sign because she was drinking a

a soda and eating a snack that she had in her hands.

Do not let others tell you to do unsafe things

that could hurt you!

They are not your friends if they do.

Please make sure that you follow the rules

and obey your parents and caring adults, so that you will not be like

Carrie Careless.

Thank goodness for Zoom-Boom coming to her rescue!

She could have gotten hurt!

So be SAFE,

pay ATTENTION,

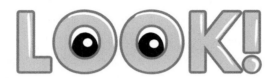

and always, BE CAREFUL!

(THE END)

About the Author Joel Brown

Joel resides in Decatur, Georgia and is an Atlanta native. He has two precious granddaughters. He loves to read bedtime stories to them. It was in these stories "Zoom-Boom" became alive. He uses his Christian beliefs to tell and share the many adventures of Zoom-Boom and his friends.

About the Illustrator Garrett Myers

Garrett resides in Albany, Georgia. He has been drawing since he was a little boy. He is gifted and talented and uses his gifts and talents to glorify God in all that he draws. He always reminds others that his drawings are creations from God, and his tools are His handiworks.

CPSIA information can be obtained
at www.ICGtesting.com
Printed in the USA
LVOW05s1028090616

491894LV00017B/95/P

9 780996 608336